A Gown for His Mistress

A FARCE IN THREE ACTS

By Georges Feydeau

Translated by Barnett Shaw

SAMUEL FRENCH, INC.
25 WEST 45TH STREET   NEW YORK 10036
7623 SUNSET BOULEVARD   HOLLYWOOD 90046
LONDON   *TORONTO*

CHARACTERS
(*In Order of Appearance*)

ETIENNE .... *butler to Moulineaux*

YVONNE .... *wife of Moulineaux*

MOULINEAUX .... *a physician*

BASSINET .... *a bore*

MADAME AIGREVILLE .... *mother of Yvonne*

SUZANNE .... *wife of Aubin*

AUBIN .... *a wealthy businessman*

MLLE. POMPINETTE. .... *a customer*

MADAME HEBERT .... *a customer*

ROSA .... *known as Madame Saint-Anigreuse*

SCENES

The action takes place in Paris at the turn of the century.

ACT ONE
Moulineaux's home-office

ACT TWO
A furnished apartment

ACT THREE
Same as Act One

3

DESCRIPTION OF CHARACTERS

ETIENNE (*Ay-tee-yen*): Any age. An efficient but stupid and rather impertinent butler.

MOULINEAUX (*Moo-lee-no*): 30 to 35. A physician and a crafty, philandering husband, instant fabricator of alibis.

BASSINET (*Bass-ee-nay*): 35 to 40. A real estate broker, blase, guileless and good-hearted fellow who never knows when he's not wanted.

AUBIN (*Oh-ban*): 40. A rather stuffy, pompous business-man.

YVONNE (*Ee-von*): 25 to 30. A pretty, gentle and naive newly-wedded wife.

SUZANNE: 25 to 30. Playful, kittenish and not too bright.

MADAME AIGREVILLE (*Egg-ruh-veal*): 50. A mother-in-law prototype, vinegary and belligerent.

ROSA: 30 to 35. A worldly woman of rather common background who puts on airs of a woman of society.

MADAME HEBERT: } customers, can be any age.
MLLE. POMPINETTE: }

NOTE: All costumes should be appropriate to 1900 France.

— Mon. — 7:00 — 10:00 — Act I
Tues. — 7:00 — 10:00 Act II
Thurs — 7:00 — 10:00 Act III

4

A Gown for His Mistress

ACT ONE

SCENE: *The living room of Doctor Moulineaux. There is a door at rear giving on a hallway. Door, Down Left, leads to Yvonne's quarters. Door, Up Left, and door, Up Right, lead to other parts of the house. Door, Down Right, leads to the quarters of Moulineaux. There is a work table at Right of Stage. Large armchair Left of table. Medical books, papers and instruments on table. Sofa at Left, as well as two chairs and a footstool.*

AT RISE: *The Stage is empty. It is early morning. ETIENNE enters at door Up Right, carrying a broom, duster, and other cleaning equipment. He yawns, lays down his equipment, sits on stool facing audience.*

ETIENNE. I'm still sleepy! Why is it that a man is always sleepiest when he gets up? People should wait until morning to go to bed. But maybe something is wrong with me. I'll have to ask the boss. That's the nice thing about working for a doctor. You can be sick for nothing. So I'm not so bad off here. But things were much better six months ago before the boss got married. Not that Madame isn't charming! I suppose if we have to have a woman around the house, this one should suit both of us. Well, it's time to wake up the doctor. You know, it's strange but his room is there— (*He points Right.*) and her room is there. (*He points Left.*) I suppose that's the way things are done in high-class society. But that's not for me! (*He knocks at door Down Right.*) Monsieur! Monsieur! He's sleeping soundly. (*Opens the door.*) Well! Nobody there!

5

The bed is still made up. Oh, ho— Monsieur didn't come home last night! He's been wandering! And his poor little wife is sleeping over there, full of trust and confidence. That's not right! But I guess that's the way those things are done in high-class society too. (YVONNE *enters from Down Left*.) Oh, Madame!

YVONNE. Is the doctor awake yet?

ETIENNE. (*Stammering*.) What? No—no—yes—yes.

YVONNE. What do you mean—no—yes? What's troubling you?

ETIENNE. Me, troubled? Do I look troubled?

YVONNE. Troubled or idiotic, I'm not sure which. (*She starts to door Down Right*.)

ETIENNE. Don't go in there!

YVONNE. What an idea! Why not?

ETIENNE. (*Very embarrassed*.) Monsieur is— Monsieur is—

YVONNE. Monsieur is what?

ETIENNE. Sick!

YVONNE. Sick? Then it's my duty to go in.

ETIENNE. No—no . . . When I said sick, I exaggerated a little. . . . He's not really sick—he's indisposed. You see, the room is full of dust. I've been sweeping in there.

YVONNE. While my husband is in bed? What are you 'rying to say?

ETIENNE. I don't know what I was trying to say, Madame, but I know I didn't say it, that's certain. (*He gives a gesture of hopelessness as* YVONNE *goes into the bedroom*.)

YVONNE. (*Coming out again*.) The bed hasn't been touched! My husband spent the night out. My compliments, Etienne. My husband must pay you well for your little services.

ETIENNE. Oh, no! I simply wanted to spare you the— (*He stops, flustered*.)

YVONNE. You're too charitable. Thanks very much. This

is frightful! After just six months of marriage. (*She goes back to her room.*)

ETIENNE. Poor little deceived woman! (*There is a KNOCK at the exterior door in the hallway.*) Who's there?

MOULINEAUX (*Offstage.*) Open the door! It's me!

ETIENNE. I'm coming! (*He opens door and* MOULINEAUX *slinks in cautiously. He is in evening clothes, his tie unknotted.*) Monsieur spent the night out?

MOULINEAUX. Sh! No! I mean—yes! Does my wife know?

ETIENNE. Your wife just went to her room, and judging by the expression on her face, I'd say . . .

MOULINEAUX. What?

ETIENNE. I'd say she knows.

MOULINEAUX. Yes? Oh, the devil!

ETIENNE. Monsieur, it was a very bad thing you did, and if you would like to trust in a friend—

MOULINEAUX. What friend?

ETIENNE. Me, Monsieur!

MOULINEAUX. Etienne, why don't you learn your place? (*He paces the floor.*) What a night! I slept on the staircase. I'll probably be stiff for a week. Oh, why did I have to go to the Opera Ball?

ETIENNE. Monsieur went to the Opera Ball?

MOULINEAUX. Yes—I mean—none of your business. Go back to the kitchen!

ETIENNE. Yes, sir!

MOULINEAUX. Never mind! Wait! Perhaps I do need someone to talk to. You'll have to do. I didn't want to go to the Opera Ball. But that pretty little devil of a Madame Aubin wanted me to go. A doctor should never have a pretty married woman for a patient—it's dangerous. "At exactly two, under the big clock," she said. What she meant was: "Wait for me until doomsday." I waited until after three o'clock—like an idiot. When I realized she wasn't going to show up, I left—furious and ready to drop. Then, when I got here, I found I had left my keys in my other clothes. I couldn't ring the bell for fear of awakening my wife. I had nothing to force the door open with. So I decided to sleep on the staircase and wait until morning. I'm stiff, sore and weary to death . . . . do you understand?

ETIENNE. At least nobody can say you were partying all night.

MOULINEAUX. Etienne, learn to have a little respect. Go to the kitchen!

ETIENNE. Yes, sir.

(*He goes out just as* YVONNE *comes out of her room*.)

YVONNE. Oh, here you are! At last!

MOULINEAUX. (*Jumping as if on a spring*.) Yes, here I am! Did you—did you sleep well, darling? You're up very early.

YVONNE. Like you.

MOULINEAUX. Me? Yes—early to bed—early to rise, that's me—when there's work to be done.

YVONNE. (*Biting out each syllable*.) WHERE DID YOU SPEND THE NIGHT?

MOULINEAUX. Huh?

YVONNE. WHERE DID YOU SPEND THE NIGHT?

MOULINEAUX. Oh, I heard you. . . . "Where did I spend—?" Didn't I tell you? Of course, I told you yesterday.

YVONNE. Told me what yesterday?

MOULINEAUX. Don't you remember? I said "I'm going to see Bassinet—he's very sick."

YVONNE. (*Incredulous*.) AND YOU SPENT THE NIGHT THERE?

MOULINEAUX. Yes—you have no idea how sick poor Bassinet is.

YVONNE. (*Bantering*.) Really!

MOULINEAUX. Yes— I had to sit up with him all night.

YVONNE. In evening clothes?

MOULINEAUX. (*Who had forgotten he had them on*.)

In evening clothes? Why, yes—of·course— I mean—no.
I'm going to explain. Bassinet is so sick that the slightest
shock or emotion will kill him. So we arranged a little get-
together—several other doctors and myself—a little get-
together in evening clothes in order to hide the true state
of affairs from poor Bassinet. You have to use subterfuge
with sick people.

YVONNE. Very ingenious. Then Bassinet is hopeless?

MOULINEAUX. Yes—the poor fellow. He'll never be up
again.

ETIENNE. (*Entering.*) Monsieur Bassinet is here!

BASSINET. (*Following* ETIENNE.) Good morning, Doctor Moulineaux.

MOULINEAUX. (*Running to him, whispering.*) Shut up
—you're sick!

BASSINET. (*Amazed.*) Who? Me? Never a day in my
life—

YVONNE. (*Sarcastic.*) Are you feeling well, Monsieur
Bassinet?

BASSINET. (*Jolly-good-fellow.*) You can see!

MOULINEAUX. (*Quickly.*) Yes—you can see he looks
very bad—he's terribly sick. (*Pushes* BASSINET *aside,
whispering.*) Are you going to shut up? You're *sick!*

YVONNE. Why do you insist on Monsieur Bassinet being
sick when he says he is—?

MOULINEAUX. What does he know about it? He's no
doctor! I tell you he's finished!

BASSINET. I'm finished—me?

MOULINEAUX. Yes, my friend—but we wanted to keep
it from you. (*Moves forward and says to audience.*) Why
doesn't he drop dead!

BASSINET. I'm finished? What did he mean?

YVONNE. It's too bad, but that's why my husband sat
up with you last night.

(MOULINEAUX *is in agony.*)

BASSINET. He sat up with me last night?

MOULINEAUX. Why, yes! Didn't you see me? (*To* YVONNE.) Leave him alone—can't you see he's delirious? (*Puts his arm on* BASSINET'S *shoulder, leads him aside, whispering.*) Please keep your big mouth shut! Can't you see you're putting your foot in it?

YVONNE. Take good care of yourself, Monsieur Bassinet. You look very well, though, for a man at death's door. You could carry on a long time.

MOULINEAUX. Oh yes, it's chronic.

YVONNE. (*Sarcastic.*) That sort of death agony is rarely fatal! (*Starts for her room.*) I think I'll speak to Mama about this! (*She goes out.*)

MOULINEAUX. Couldn't you see that you were making one blunder after another? Haven't you sense enough to understand anything?

BASSINET. Understand what?

MOULINEAUX. The situation—the horrible situation!

BASSINET. What situation?

MOULINEAUX. If I put you at death's door, I had my reason. Couldn't you stay there? Why did you barge in here in the first place?

BASSINET. Barge in? What?

MOULINEAUX. Couldn't you have had the tact not to come?

BASSINET. How was I to guess?

MOULINEAUX. Name of a cow, the morning after the Opera Ball you don't visit people who have used you as an excuse for going out.

BASSINET. But why didn't you tell me?

MOULINEAUX. Does someone have to dot every "I" for you?

BASSINET. Well, it would be normal.

MOULINEAUX. What do you want, anyhow?

BASSINET. Well—this is what I wanted. . . . You know I never come unless there's a service to be rendered.

MOULINEAUX. Oh, you want me to do you a service?

BASSINET. No—I want to do you one.

MOULINEAUX. Well—that's better. The other way

around would be more normal. But you'll have to pardon me. I'm very tired. I slept on the staircase. (*He sinks into the sofa.*)

BASSINET. That's all right—don't mind me. (*He sits also.*)

MOULINEAUX. But I'm expecting my mother-in-law any moment—and you understand—

BASSINET. Yes, I understand. Here's what I wanted to tell you—

MOULINEAUX. (*Gets up and rings.*) Pardon me please.

ETIENNE. (*Coming in.*) You rang, Monsieur?

MOULINEAUX. (*In whisper.*) Yes. Get rid of this man. In five minutes bring me a visiting card—any old card—and tell me that someone wants to talk to me. That will give him the hint to leave.

ETIENNE. The usual treatment for bores—I understand, sir. (*He exits.*)

BASSINET. You know, it's a year since I got my inheritance.

MOULINEAUX. Your inheritance?

BASSINET. (*Getting up.*) Yes, from my uncle. Well, I bought a building at Number Seventy, Rue de Milan. Now, my apartments are not rented so I thought it would be of great service to you if you would interest some of your patients in renting them. (*Hands him a brochure.*)

MOULINEAUX. (*Furious, walks Downstage.*) You came in here and bothered me about that?

BASSINET. Don't get angry. You have nothing to lose. My apartments are very unhealthy. I'll increase your clientele.

MOULINEAUX. Oh, go to the devil. Do you think I'm going to recommend your unsanitary apartments to my patients?

BASSINET. But I have one that's a gem—all furnished—a bargain. A dressmaker had it but she left without paying her rent. It's a very funny story—you see, this dress-maker—she—

MOULINEAUX. I don't care a rap about your dressmaker or your apartment or your story. What do you want me to do with your dressmaker?

BASSINET. It's not the dressmaker I'm interested in—

MOULINEAUX. I know. But you could have picked a better time to talk to me about it. When I think that all this time my poor wife—

BASSINET. You're lucky to have a wife. I lost mine.

MOULINEAUX. Good! That's very good!

BASSINET. What do you mean—"That's good"?

MOULINEAUX. I meant to say—"That's too bad—too bad." (*Crosses to Right.*)

BASSINET. Imagine. She was carried away in the space of five minutes.

MOULINEAUX. By a heart attack?

BASSINET. No—by a soldier. I left her on a park bench. I said to her: "Wait for me, I'm going across the street to get a cigar." I never found her again.

(*A BELL rings.*)

MOULINEAUX. Pardon me, someone is ringing.

ETIENNE. (*He enters.*) A gentleman says he must talk to you, sir. Here's his card.

MOULINEAUX. Oh, yes. (*To* BASSINET.) Please pardon me, Bassinet—there's someone to see me. He's a bore but I can't very well put him off.

BASSINET. A bore? I know that type. Let him come in. When he sees that you're busy with me, he'll leave. (*He sits.*)

MOULINEAUX. But he wants to speak to me privately.

BASSINET. Oh, that's another matter. What's the bore's name? (*Takes the card from* MOULINEAUX'S *hand.*) Oh, Dubois. I know him very well. I'll be delighted to shake his hand again. I'll leave afterwards.

MOULINEAUX. No—you can't do that. It's not the Dubois that you think. It's his father.

BASSINET. He never had a father.

MOULINEAUX. Then it's his uncle—that's right—his uncle. And he doesn't want to be seen. Please go. (*Helps him out of the chair.*)

BASSINET. Very well. (*He starts to door at rear as if he is about to leave, then quickly slips towards the door Up Right.*) I'll just wait in the other room. (*He goes out.*)

MOULINEAUX. Won't he ever leave! Well, never mind! I'll keep him waiting in there the rest of the day.

BASSINET. (*Reappearing.*) I just had an idea. If that bore gets too bothersome, I'll ring and then I'll send in my card and you can tell him it's some bore you must talk to.

MOULINEAUX. Good, good! You do that. But go in there! You'll find a couch. You can sleep if you're tired. (BASSINET *leaves.*) At last! That was a lot of trouble. (*He sinks into a chair.*)

ETIENNE. I beg your pardon, but since you are a doctor you should use the means at your disposal to get rid of intruders.

MOULINEAUX. I thought he'd never go.

ETIENNE. If I were in your place I would use chloroform.

MOULINEAUX. It's not that serious, Etienne. It's just that I've been upset on account of all that happened this morning. I'm going to try to sleep for an hour. Please don't let anyone disturb me. (*He stretches out on the sofa.*)

ETIENNE. Very well, sir.

MOULINEAUX. (*With eyes closed.*) This feels good. I won't be long in falling to sleep.

ETIENNE. When shall I call you, sir?

MOULINEAUX. Tomorrow—or the day after—but not if I'm sleeping.

ETIENNE. Very well. One of these days, then! Good day, sir.

MOULINEAUX. (*Half asleep.*) Good day. (ETIENNE *exits.*)

(*There is a pause while* MOULINEAUX *sleeps, then a BELL rings and we hear a NOISE Offstage.*)

MME. AIGREVILLE. (*Offstage.*) I WANT TO SEE MY DAUGHTER AND MY SON-IN-LAW!

ETIENNE. (*Entering like a bomb.*) Monsieur, your mother-in-law is here. (*Goes to the door of* YVONNE'S *room.*) Madame, your mother is here!

MME. AIGREVILLE. (*Bursting in, suitcase in hand.*) My children! My children!

YVONNE. (*Entering.*) Mama!

MOULINEAUX. (*Jumping up from sofa.*) What was that —a cyclone? (*Dazed.*) My mother-in-law! What a way to be awakened!

MME. AIGREVILLE. (*Kissing* YVONNE.) My dear daughter! (*To* MOULINEAUX.) Well, aren't you going to kiss me?

MOULINEAUX. I was going to ask you that. You know how it is—the surprise and the shock—when a person goes to sleep without a mother-in-law and wakes up with one. It takes a moment to get over it. Kiss me, mother-in-law. (*He closes his eyes, sticks out his face to be kissed. She puts her arm around his head as she kisses him.*) Don't shake me too much, I'm not quite awake yet.

MME. AIGREVILLE. Have you been sleeping?

MOULINEAUX. Very little.

MME. AIGREVILLE. You look to me as if you've slept too much. (*Bursting into tears.*) Oh, my dear children, I'm so happy to see you.

MOULINEAUX. Careful! You'll get yourself wet.

YVONNE. Don't cry, Mama.

MME. AIGREVILLE. (*Sobbing.*) I'm not crying. It's just my emotion at seeing you again. Oh, Moulineaux, you're getting thin. He's getting thin, Yvonne . . . but you look fine. Moulineaux, why are you wearing that black suit? Are you going to a funeral?

MOULINEAUX. Yes—it's for you.

MME. AIGREVILLE. What?

MOULINEAUX. I mean—it's in your honor.

YVONNE. He's been sitting up with one of his patients who is chronically dead.

MME. AIGREVILLE. Are you a night doctor now?

MOULINEAUX. Oh, no, but when there's the Opera— (*Catching himself.*) operations or emergencies—a doctor must do his duty.

YVONNE. Even if it takes all night long.

MME. AIGREVILLE. You sound a little bitter towards your husband. Have you been quarreling?

MOULINEAUX. Oh, no. Sometimes people wake up in a bad humor.

YVONNE. And sometimes they never go to bed at all.

MME. AIGREVILLE. Now, now, don't get upset. I'm here! There's nothing like a mother-in-law to prevent discord between young newlyweds.

ETIENNE. (*Entering with card.*) Monsieur, here's a card that the gentleman of a while ago asked me to give you.

MOULINEAUX. (*Looks at card.*) From Bassinet! Oh, no! Tell him I've had enough of him for a month.

MME. AIGREVILLE. What is it?

MOULINEAUX. Oh, nothing important. Etienne, will you get my doctor's robe and bring it to me.

ETIENNE. Yes, sir. (*He exits.*)

BASSINET. (*Entering.*) I say there, did you know I'm still here?

MOULINEAUX. (*Pushing him back into the room.*) Get back in there—*please!*

MME. AIGREVILLE. Who was that?

MOULINEAUX. A patient—a very sick man.

MME. AIGREVILLE. Why did you chase him out of here?

MOULINEAUX. He has a very contagious disease.

MME. AIGREVILLE. Really?

MOULINEAUX. The most contagious—and once you have it you can't get rid of it.

YVONNE. (*Sarcastic.*) It's a very accommodating disease, however.

MOULINEAUX. Another rock in my garden!

MME. AIGREVILLE. Something is going on and I want to know what it is. Moulineaux, will you please leave me with my daughter? I should like to speak to her.

MOULINEAUX. Oh, with pleasure—especially when my wife is in such a mood. (*He goes out Right.*)

MME. AIGREVILLE. (*Sitting on sofa.*) Well now—tell me —what is it you have against your husband?

YVONNE. (*In tears, sits next to her mother.*) Mama— I'm so unhappy!

MME. AIGREVILLE. My God! What is it?

YVONNE. My husband didn't come home last night. And maybe other nights that I know nothing about.

MME. AIGREVILLE. (*Astonished.*) That you know nothing about? It seems to me you would know—especially at night.

YVONNE. How would I know?

MME. AIGREVILLE. How? If he left your bedroom. Where is your bedroom?

YVONNE. Which one? Mine?

MME. AIGREVILLE. What do you mean—yours?

YVONNE. Mine is there—and his is there.

MME. AIGREVILLE. After six months of marriage— you're there—and he's there?

YVONNE. It's always been like that.

MME. AIGREVILLE. But that's all wrong—very wrong. The double bed is the safeguard of conjugal happiness.

YVONNE. Yes?

MME. AIGREVILLE. Of course! It's what strengthens the marriage bonds. It's elementary—it's plain arithmetic— it's as simple as one plus one equals one.

BASSINET. (*Entering.*) Pardon me, Madame.

MME. AIGREVILLE. (*Taking refuge behind a chair.*) Good God! The contagious one! Will you go back where you came from?

BASSINET. I wanted to speak to Doctor Moulineaux.

YVONNE. To arrange another little deal with him no

doubt? It's a very pretty profession you have there, sir. There's a name for it!

BASSINET. (*Amazed.*) Huh? But I— (*Takes a step towards* MADAME AIGREVILLE.)

MME. AIGREVILLE. (*Running from him.*) Go away—go away. Go to bed where you belong.

BASSINET. (*He advances on her.*) Why should I go to bed?

MME. AIGREVILLE. (*Going around chair to avoid him.*) When you're sick you should stay in bed. Go away! Go to bed!

BASSINET. I don't know what's wrong with everyone. I never felt better in my life. Will you please tell Doctor Moulineaux—

MME. AIGREVILLE. (*Gesturing for him to leave.*) You—you—all right—I'll tell him.

BASSINET. I thank you. May I kiss your hand?

MME. AIGREVILLE. Heavens no! Good-bye! Good-bye!

BASSINET. Good-bye, madame. (*He exits at door Up Right.*)

MME. AIGREVILLE. It's disgusting the way your husband allows contagious people to roam around. Now, dear, you were saying that your husband spent the night out?

YVONNE. All the way out, Mama. And I'm so unhappy.

MME. AIGREVILLE. Don't cry. Explain this to me first. For whom has your husband given up your bed?

YVONNE. For whom?

MME. AIGREVILLE. Name of a name! A husband doesn't stay out all night to look at the stars. Have you any clues?

YVONNE. (*Taking a woman's glove from her pocket.*) I don't know. Yesterday I found this glove in his pocket.

MME. AIGREVILLE. A woman's glove. That's a clue! Have you read his mail?

YVONNE. Oh, I would never do that.

MME. AIGREVILLE. But how else will you know who writes to him? All women read their husbands' mail. (MOULINEAUX *enters.*) Let me talk to him. Go to your room. MOULINEAUX!

MOULINEAUX. Yes, mother of my dear wife.

MME. AIGREVILLE. I won't beat around the bush. Do you recognize this glove?

MOULINEAUX. Yes! I've been looking everywhere for it. (*He starts to take it but she slaps his hand with it.*)

MME. AIGREVILLE. Don't touch! Whose glove is this?

MOULINEAUX. Huh? Whose? Why—it's mine.

MME. AIGREVILLE. YOURS? A size like this?

MOULINEAUX. It's to strengthen my hand for operations. You see, when I have it on, I exercise my fingers like this. (*He wiggles his fingers frantically.*)

MME. AIGREVILLE. Such a story! THIS IS A WOMAN'S GLOVE!

MOULINEAUX. It looks like it, doesn't it? It got wet and it shrunk.

MME. AIGREVILLE. (*Showing the glove in its full elbow length.*) AND WHAT ABOUT THE LENGTH?

MOULINEAUX. Precisely! It shrunk and it stretched. It was the water that did it. What it lost in width, it gained in length. It's a law of physics. For example, if you were to get wet, you would— (*He makes a wide stretching motion.*)

MME. AIGREVILLE. But just look here—it's marked six and a half.

MOULINEAUX. Nine and a half. The water made the numbers run in reverse.

MME. AIGREVILLE. MOULINEAUX, DO YOU TAKE ME FOR AN IDIOT?

MOULINEAUX. Not altogether.

MME. AIGREVILLE. Let me tell you that you are an abominable husband—a debauched philanderer.

MOULINEAUX. Me?

MME. AIGREVILLE. Yes—debauched! You stay out all night—you have women's gloves in your pocket.

MOULINEAUX. I told you it was wet.

MME. AIGREVILLE. Yes, you told me. Well, LET ME TELL YOU—if you deceive my daughter, you will have me to deal with.

MOULINEAUX. It will be a pleasure.

MME. AIGREVILLE. You know that you are married and that you swore fidelity.

MOULINEAUX. Yes—but not to you!

MME. AIGREVILLE. You know that under the law a wife follows her husband, consequently, WE shall follow you.

MOULINEAUX. I beg your pardon. . . . The law says the wife, but not the mother-in-law.

MME. AIGREVILLE. Unnatural man! Would you separate a daughter from her mother?

MOULINEAUX. Oh, GO TO THE DEVIL!

MME. AIGREVILLE. WHAT DID YOU SAY?

MOULINEAUX. You've come here to plague me! Let me tell you that I am the master in my house and I am accountable to no one, especially not to you. WHY DON'T YOU GO TAKE A WALK?

MME. AIGREVILLE. And they say that mother-in-laws start things! I think you would like me to believe that I am not wanted here. (*She starts to the rear.*)

MOULINEAUX. Well, if you're going to cause trouble.

MME. AIGREVILLE. That's right—throw me out—throw me out of my daughter's house. I'll leave—you won't have to tell me twice.

MOULINEAUX. Never mind! I'll leave myself. Madame, you exasperate me and you would exasperate a saint. (*He exits quickly at Right.*)

MME. AIGREVILLE. They're all alike. My husband treated my dear mother the same way. I won't spend the night here. I'll find a refuge somewhere.

BASSINET. (*Who has opened the door.*) What you need is a furnished apartment. I have just the thing.

MME. AIGREVILLE. (*Frightened.*) Oh—the contagious man!

BASSINET. I have a nice little apartment at 70 Rue de Milan—all furnished.

MME. AIGREVILLE. (*With anxiety.*) Did you ever live there?

BASSINET. No, it was a dressmaker. There's a funny story about her. Can you imagine? This dressmaker—

MME. AIGREVILLE. Never mind! Is the apartment sanitary?

BASSINET. That depends. Is it to live in?

MME. AIGREVILLE. What do you mean?

BASSINET. Sometimes people rent apartments for other purposes.

MME. AIGREVILLE. Sir!

BASSINET. In your case—it's sanitary—like all apartments.

MME. AIGREVILLE. We'll visit it today.

BASSINET. I'll get things straightened up.

(MOULINEAUX *enters.*)

MME. AIGREVILLE. I leave the house to you, my son-in-law. (*She goes out.*)

MOULINEAUX. (*Seeing* BASSINET.) I've been thinking about that apartment of yours. I'd like to rent it.

BASSINET. Yes?

MOULINEAUX. I have a particular need for it. I can tell you, because I know you won't talk. I'm having an affair —still platonic, but I have hopes to change all that. She's a married woman—one of my patients.

BASSINET. What's wrong with her?

MOULINEAUX. Nothing—I cured her weeks ago.

BASSINET. And what about her husband?

MOULINEAUX. I've never seen him. But no matter—how much is your apartment?

BASSINET. Two hundred and fifty.

MOULINEAUX. A year? That's a bargain. I'll take it.

BASSINET. No—no—two hundred and fifty a month.

MOULINEAUX. Raising the rent already, eh? But I'll take it, just the same.

BASSINET. When?

MOULINEAUX. Today, of course.

BASSINET. (*Mechanically twisting Moulineaux's lapels.*)

The devil! It's still in topsy-turvy shape—dressmaker gadgets everywhere. You see, I told you it was rented by a dressmaker. Let me tell you a funny story about her. It seems she—

MOULINEAUX. Tomorrow—tell me the story tomorrow.

BASSINET. But the apartment is not in order yet.

MOULINEAUX. That makes no difference. It will do for today. You can put it in shape later.

ETIENNE. (*He enters.*) Monsieur, Madame Aubin is here.

MOULINEAUX. Good! (*To* BASSINET.) Go in there and draw up the papers. (*He pushes* BASSINET *into the next room. To* ETIENNE.) Oh, you have my robe.

(SUZANNE *enters gaily.*)

SUZANNE. Bonjour, my dear!

MOULINEAUX. Oh, here you are! (*To* ETIENNE *who is holding out the doctor's white robe.*) Later—later—not now. Wear it yourself, with my compliments. (*To* SUZANNE.) Why did you stand me up at the Opera Ball?

(ETIENNE *exits.*)

SUZANNE. Darling, I'm sick about that. I hoped that my husband would roam around during the evening but he stayed glued to my side until the silly ball was over.

MOULINEAUX. I was afraid that was the reason.

SUZANNE. For several days he's been going everywhere with me. He has spells like that. Right now he's waiting for me downstairs. He wanted to come up but I insisted that he stay there.

MOULINEAUX. That was wise. I'm not anxious to make his acquaintance. (*Amorous, he draws her to the sofa.*) My dear little Suzanne.

SUZANNE. Oh, Moulineaux, I'm very wicked to listen to you.

MOULINEAUX. Not at all. Don't you believe that.

SUZANNE. It's too late to worry about it now, isn't it?

MOULINEAUX. Much too late, my dear Suzanne.

SUZANNE. You know this is the first time I've ever done anything like this.

MOULINEAUX. (*Bored at the thought.*) Yes, you've told me that before. (*Changing his tone.*) And it gave me an exquisite sense of joy. But listen to me. We can't see each other here any longer. The consultations were a good pretext but they can't go on forever. Someone will notice how frequently you come here and they will eventually learn the truth. (*Glowing.*) They will know that we are not doctor and patient but two hearts deeply in love, two souls on a flight to the tender gardens of passion.

SUZANNE. That would nip our wick, wouldn't it?

MOULINEAUX. How cleverly you put it! Well, if you are willing, we can see each other this very day—on neutral ground.

SUZANNE. On the ground? I would rather have a nice little apartment.

MOULINEAUX. That's what I mean. I have a little place—70 Rue de Milan. We'll meet there. It's already furnished.

SUZANNE. It's tempting. But you must give me your word. . . . Our love must remain—uh—what was that word you used once—symphonic?

MOULINEAUX. Platonic.

SUZANNE. That's it! That's the way it must be. Because you know I'm true to my husband.

MOULINEAUX. Of course you are. Who would ever question that? (*He draws her near and kisses her.*)

SUZANNE. Then it's all arranged—in one hour at 70 Rue de Milan. Oh, this is terribly wrong, and you know it's the first time for me.

MOULINEAUX. Of course—of course. You told me.

SUZANNE. I did? (*She starts to leave.*) In an hour then.

(ETIENNE *enters with doctor's robe on.*)

ETIENNE. Monsieur Aubin is here.

SUZANNE. My husband!

MOULINEAUX. But I don't want to see him.

(AUBIN *enters.*)

SUZANNE. I was just coming down.

AUBIN. (*In a brisk manner.*) Good, good. I'll join you in a moment. (*Notices* MOULINEAUX *in black suit, tosses his topcoat to him.*) Leave us, please. (*To* ETIENNE.) Doctor!

MOULINEAUX. (*Amazed.*) Huh! Oh, I see—this is good.

SUZANNE. (*To* AUBIN.) But, my dear—

MOULINEAUX. Sh! Let it go—I like this. (*He steers her to the door and she exits. Then he goes out at Right.*)

AUBIN. While I was downstairs, I said to myself that I might as well consult you while I'm here. I've been troubled with frequent nosebleeds.

ETIENNE. Yes? Well, use your dining room key.

AUBIN. The dining room key?

ETIENNE. Whenever possible—the dining room key. Put it in your—in your back.

AUBIN. The dining room key?

ETIENNE. Yes. And keep your nose and mouth in a bucket of cold water for an hour and a half.

AUBIN. Should I breathe?

ETIENNE. Of course—breathe—provided that you keep your mouth and nose in the water. That's all. That will cure you—in an hour and a half.

AUBIN. Well, I would prefer another cure. But aren't you going to look at my tongue? What do you think? (*Sticks out his tongue.*)

ETIENNE. Mine is longer. (*He sticks out his tongue.*)

AUBIN. Huh?

ETIENNE. Yours is round and mine is pointed. (*Sticks tongue out again.*)

AUBIN. Yes, Doctor—I see.

ETIENNE. I'm not the doctor.

AUBIN. Not the doctor?

ETIENNE. I'm his butler.

AUBIN. His butler—and you converse with me?

ETIENNE. I'm not proud—and besides, I didn't have anything better to do.

AUBIN. But who was the one that took my coat?

(*At this moment* BASSINET *enters with* MOULINEAUX *who has changed into an ordinary suit.*)

MOULINEAUX. I'm ready to go.

BASSINET. Here is your lease.

MOULINEAUX. Thank you, my friend.

BASSINET. By the way, I didn't finish that story. You see, this dressmaker—

MOULINEAUX. Later, later—right now I have pleasure on my mind. (*He goes to door but* AUBIN *intercepts him.*)

AUBIN. Pardon me, Doctor.

MOULINEAUX. I'm not the doctor. (*He goes out quickly.*)

AUBIN. Oh—that was a patient. (*Seeing* BASSINET.) This is the doctor. Monsieur, I stayed to make my excuses.

BASSINET. (*Smoothing his hat, turns to see who is addressing him.*) Your excuses?

AUBIN. Yes, on account of my coat. I thought I was giving it to the butler but it was a patient.

BASSINET. (*Not comprehending.*) Huh? Well, it's of no importance. Let me tell you about this dressmaker who rented my apartment. She—

AUBIN. (*Who goes to door with* BASSINET *trailing him.*) Very interesting—but you must pardon me. It's been a pleasure. (*He exits.*)

BASSINET. Everybody is leaving. Ah—the butler! (*To* ETIENNE.) I'm going to tell you a good story.

ETIENNE. I have things to do in the kitchen.

BASSINET. (*Not listening, sits.*) But wait a moment. You see, this dressmaker had a boy friend who was—(BASSINET *laughs.* ETIENNE *profits by fact that* BASSINET *is not looking at him and tip-toes out the door.* BASSINET *realizes he has gone and looks into each door to see where he went, finally resigns himself to being alone and goes to the front of the Stage and talks to the audience.*) You see—this dressmaker who rented my apartment had a boy friend. (*He laughs heartily.*) This boy friend . . .

(*He can't refrain from another laugh. The* CURTAIN *comes down and cuts him short.*)

END OF ACT ONE

ACT TWO

SCENE: *Apartment at 70 Rue de Milan, one flight above the street. Rear door, which has a broken lock, opens on a staircase landing visible to the audience. A chair is at each side of the entrance door. At Left, not far from the door, a mannikin with a woman's dress. Door at Left, window at Right. A sofa is at Right; at Left is a table on which are many accoutrements of a dressmaker.*

AT RISE: MOULINEAUX *comes in and surveys the place.*

MOULINEAUX. Not bad—not bad. This should serve the purpose very well. (*Rubs his hands together.*) And this in particular! (*He gives the sofa a thump.*) Very nice indeed! (*He tries the door.*) The devil! The lock is broken. Fine thing for a lover's hideaway! I'll give Bassinet my comments on that! (*As he turns, he finds himself face to face with the mannikin.*) I beg your pardon! Oh, it's a dummy! (*Pats the mannikin on the cheek.*) Don't tell a soul what you see here, chérie.

(SUZANNE *enters at rear.*)

SUZANNE. It's me!

MOULINEAUX. Suzanne—my pet!

SUZANNE. The door won't lock.

MOULINEAUX. I'll take care of that. I'll put up a barricade. (*He places a chair against the door.*)

SUZANNE. But someone could still come in. Isn't there any danger?

MOULINEAUX. (*Advancing on her, sensuously.*) What danger would you like, my sweet? We're all alone. Sit here

26

with me. (*He pulls her to the sofa, sits with her, holds her hands.*) Don't tremble like that.

SUZANNE. I'll get over it. My husband was a soldier once and he said that even the bravest men shake when they go under fire for the first time.

MOULINEAUX. He said that? Bravo! But I'm not going to shoot you. Take off your hat.

SUZANNE. Oh, no! I can't stay but a moment. Anatole is downstairs. He might come up.

MOULINEAUX. Anatole?

SUZANNE. Yes—my husband. He still wants to go everywhere with me.

MOULINEAUX. You mean he knows you are here with me?

SUZANNE. Yes.

MOULINEAUX. Good God!

SUZANNE. No—I don't mean what you think. I told him I was going to see my dressmaker. You told me a dressmaker used to live here. That's what gave me the idea.

MOULINEAUX. Well—that's better. You had me trembling too.

SUZANNE. I know it's bothersome to have him go with me, but if I had refused he would have been suspicious. And besides, I didn't want to stand you up.

MOULINEAUX. For the second time, you mean? I understand, dear Suzanne. (*Distracted, he keeps looking at the door while he talks.*) My dear little Suzanne. My dear little Suzanne.

SUZANNE. You already said that.

MOULINEAUX. Did I? (*Still looking at door.*) My dear little Suzanne.

SUZANNE. That makes four times.

MOULINEAUX. Four times—yes! My dear little—

SUZANNE. I'm being very sinful I think.

MOULINEAUX. Oh, no—no—no.

SUZANNE. You know this is the first time for me.

MOULINEAUX. (*Mechanically.*) Really?

SUZANNE. I swear it. Are you happy to have me here?

MOULINEAUX. What! Am I happy? Am I *happy!* (*He hums, completely distracted, strolling around.*) Two hundred and fifty a month! And her husband is downstairs!

SUZANNE. What are you thinking about?

MOULINEAUX. Nothing, nothing—I mean—I'm thinking of you.

SUZANNE. You seem very cold and distant. I'm sure that you despise me.

MOULINEAUX. Suzanne—how can you say that? I want to spend my life at your knees.

SUZANNE. You say that, but—

MOULINEAUX. The proof! (*He gets down on his knees and clasps her around the waist.*)

(AUBIN *enters, pushing the chair aside.*)

AUBIN. I seem to be knocking everything down.

MOULINEAUX. You can't come in!

AUBIN. What? I can't come in?

MOULINEAUX. You misunderstood. I said, "Please come in!"

AUBIN. Thank you. I'm already in. I got bored downstairs and decided to come up.

MOULINEAUX. An excellent idea.

AUBIN. But don't let me disturb you. Carry on as if I weren't here.

MOULINEAUX. That's easy to say.

AUBIN. Please go on. I see you're taking my wife's measurements.

SUZANNE. (*Grasping at the idea.*) That's right! He was measuring my waist.

MOULINEAUX. (*He assumes an effeminate manner which he continues to use whenever* AUBIN *is present.*) Yes—of course—the waist—let's see— (*He puts his hands around her waist.*) Fifty-five!

SUZANNE. What do you mean, fifty-five? I'm twenty-two.

AUBIN. That's correct—twenty-two.

MOULINEAUX. Twenty-two is the old way of counting. Ordinary dressmakers still use it, but high class couturiers use a new system—it's based on trigonometry—the numbers are much larger but it all comes out the same.

AUBIN. The bills are much larger too, I suppose. (*He laughs*.)

MOULINEAUX. Much, much larger. That's what distinguishes us from the little dressmakers. And we work with the eye—no tape measures.

AUBIN. Very original, Monsieur. . . . Monsieur—what is your name?

(MOULINEAUX *can only gurgle*.)

SUZANNE. Monsieur— (*She can't think of a name*.)

AUBIN. I didn't quite catch the name—what was it?

MOULINEAUX. (*Another gurgle*.) I have something in my throat. The name is Blob—Alexis Blob.

AUBIN. I've heard that name somewhere.

MOULINEAUX. My father was a Blob. My grandfather was a very famous Blob. My aunt—

AUBIN. Of course. But your face is familiar to me too. Where have I seen you before?

MOULINEAUX. (*Trying vainly to disguise his face and voice*.) I have no idea. . . . In a museum, I suspect. I go there to study fashions through the ages.

AUBIN. But I never go to museums. I know where it was—it was at my wife's physician—Doctor Moulineaux. I ran into you there. Does he take care of you?

MOULINEAUX. A little—very little, if you must know.

AUBIN. I agree. He's a quack.

MOULINEAUX. How can you say such a thing?

AUBIN. What does it matter to you?

MOULINEAUX. He's my doctor and I have his interest at heart.

AUBIN. You're very loyal. Well, I was only joking, after all. (*Sits on chair facing* MOULINEAUX.) Tell me—what did you have in mind for my wife?

MOULINEAUX. (*Not realizing the meaning.*) Me? Oh—nothing—nothing.

AUBIN. But you're making something for her.

MOULINEAUX. OH! YES! An evening gown . . . something very chic . . . leopard skin with tufts of zebra around the waist . . . ornamented with jade and ivory. The pants will be made of real mink.

AUBIN. Pants?

MOULINEAUX. You won't see them of course—they're underneath. But mink is very luxurious—especially when it's hidden.

AUBIN. I hope the design is not too extreme.

MOULINEAUX. It's the latest—in fact, it's years ahead. It's the "wild look"—inspired by Africa—safaris, jungle drums and all that sort of thing.

(POMPINETTE *comes in.*)

POMPINETTE. Is Madame Durand here?

MOULINEAUX. Madame Durand? (*Puzzled, he looks at* SUZANNE.) No . . . she's not here.

POMPINETTE. I wanted to see her about my bill.

MOULINEAUX. The bill? What bill?

POMPINETTE. The bill for the dress she made for me.

MOULINEAUX. Of course, of course—you mean Madame Durand, the dressmaker. I thought you meant Madame Durand, the cleaning woman. It's very confusing, you see. But you mean Madame Durand, my associate for all these years.

POMPINETTE. If you're her associate, I can talk to you. I am Mademoiselle Pompinette.

MOULINEAUX. I'm glad to hear that.

POMPINETTE. I'd like a reduction in my bill. The dress should not have been as much as Madame Durand charged me.

MOULINEAUX. How much was it?

POMPINETTE. Three hundred and forty. That's an enormous amount for such a simple little dress.

MOULINEAUX. I agree. How much reduction would you like?

POMPINETTE. It seems to me that three hundred would be about right.

MOULINEAUX. That sounds reasonable. So we'll take off three hundred. That leaves forty. Is that satisfactory?

POMPINETTE. But I meant—

MOULINEAUX. Now, now—I insist. We strive to please our customers. We want you to come back. SOME OTHER TIME!

POMPINETTE. Thank you. I really didn't expect such a generous reduction. I'll be back.

MOULINEAUX. Good day, Mademoiselle.

(POMPINETTE *exits*.)

AUBIN. (*Aside.*) What fantastic profits they must make here! (*To* MOULINEAUX.) I must go too. I leave my wife in your hands. Take good care of her. See if you can do something clever for her hips and bust, won't you?

MOULINEAUX. I'll do my best.

AUBIN. Au revoir, Monsieur. (*He exits.*)

MOULINEAUX. (*Placing chair against the door.*) At last! He's gone. (*He sits on the chair.*)

SUZANNE. We're in a terrible mess. What are we going to do?

MOULINEAUX. I know what I'm going to do. I'm going to get out of here as quickly as possible.

SUZANNE. But you can't do that! My husband thinks you're my dressmaker and he may come back here. If he doesn't find you, he'll guess the truth. And I know him— HE'LL KILL YOU.

MOULINEAUX. HE CAN'T DO THAT! HE'S NO DOCTOR! Oh, Suzanne, what a predicament.

(BASSINET *bursts through the door, causing* MOULINEAUX *to fall off the chair and roll towards the sofa.* BASSINET *bumps into the chair.*)

BASSINET. What's going on here?

MOULINEAUX. (*Half crouched on the floor.*) Is that a way to come into a room?

BASSINET. Why must you sit against the door?

MOULINEAUX. Because the blasted thing won't lock, that's why! What kind of run-down apartment did you rent me?

BASSINET. I warned you. You could at least have given me an hour to put it in order.

MOULINEAUX. But who ever heard of locks that don't lock? A man can walk in here as easily as into his own bathroom—any idiot who happens along.

BASSINET. You mean me?

MOULINEAUX. It fits!

BASSINET. Don't worry, I'll write to the locksmith. I had to force the door open after the dressmaker left without giving me the keys.

MOULINEAUX. All right, all right! But for the moment, can't you see that I'm not alone? (*He indicates* SUZANNE *who has turned her back to him, Up Left.*)

BASSINET. Oh, Madame! I beg your pardon. I didn't see you. But don't worry—you're not in the way. I have no secrets. Don't leave on my account.

MOULINEAUX. You have your full share of gall, my friend.

(*At this moment* MADAME HEBERT *comes in the rear door.*)

MME. HEBERT. Pardon me, I'd like to see Madame Durand, if you please.

MOULINEAUX. Another one!

MME. HEBERT. I came to see about this jacket.

MOULINEAUX. Not today—come back next week. (*Advancing on* MADAME HEBERT.) I don't care that much about your jacket! (*He snaps his fingers in her face.*)

MME. HEBERT. (*Stiffening.*) Well! I WON'T PAY FOR IT—THAT'S ALL! I DON'T CARE!

MOULINEAUX. NOR DO I!!!

MME. HEBERT. You're very courteous to your clients in this establishment! (*She leaves in a huff.*)

SUZANNE. (*Low to* MOULINEAUX.) Can't you make him leave?

(MOULINEAUX *advances on* BASSINET *but it doesn't prevent him from talking.*)

BASSINET. Let me tell you what a shock I had. I thought I was on the trail of my wife. Somebody told me that a Madame Bassinet was living near here.

MOULINEAUX. Tell me about it later.

BASSINET. No—listen. (*To* SUZANNE.) You can listen too, Madame—no secrets. You see, it wasn't my wife, but someone I had never seen before. I said to her: "I beg your pardon, I was looking for a woman." And do you know what she said to me? She said: "Do I look like a giraffe?" How do you like that? To tell you the truth—she did look like a giraffe.

(MADAME AIGREVILLE *comes to the door,* MOULINEAUX *grabs* SUZANNE *and tries to get her out of sight.*)

MME. AIGREVILLE. (*Seeing* BASSINET.) Oh—the contagious man! I came to see your apartment.

BASSINET. I'm sorry but it's rented.

MME. AIGREVILLE. Why didn't you tell me so? (*Turning, she sees* MOULINEAUX.) My son-in-law!

MOULINEAUX. Here I am, mother-in-law.

MME. AIGREVILLE. What are you doing here? I have the right to know.

MOULINEAUX. But—but—

MME. AIGREVILLE. So you refuse to talk? Take care— I have the right to be suspicious.

MOULINEAUX. Of what? I've come to see a patient—a sick woman.

MME. AIGREVILLE. Indeed!

MOULINEAUX. (*Making desperate gestures to* SU-
ZANNE.) Isn't it true, Madame, that you are my patient?

MME. AIGREVILLE. (*Very agreeable.*) My dear lady, I
didn't doubt it for a moment.

SUZANNE. (*Playing her role as mistress of the house.*)
And may I know to whom I have the honor of speaking?

MOULINEAUX. (*Interceding.*) This is Madame Aigreville, my mother-in-law. This is Madame Aubin—Madame
Suzanne Aubin.

MME. AIGREVILLE. Is my son-in-law treating you?

SUZANNE. Very well—I mean—yes, he's treating me—
and my husband also.

MME. AIGREVILLE. I'm happy that he's taking care of
you both. What does your husband have?

MOULINEAUX. (*Quickly.*) Dermatitis—the worst kind—
impetiginous dermatitis—caused by a confinement.

MME. AIGREVILLE. Confinement? Her husband?

MOULINEAUX. Not him—his wife.

SUZANNE. Me?

MME. AIGREVILLE. You're a mother, then?

SUZANNE. No—not at all.

MOULINEAUX. (*Stammering it out.*) Not her—him!
You see—it was very strange. Her husband imagined it all.
Then when he learned that it wasn't so—you see—the
emotion—the regret—his blood circulated too fast and he
broke out with dermatitis—impetiginous dermatitis—in
both the upper and lower vestibules.

MME. AIGREVILLE. Both vestibules? That's dreadful!

MOULINEAUX. And now, I'd like for you to leave me
with my patient.

MME. AIGREVILLE. Of course. I'll be going. If my
daughter comes, will you tell her that I have left?

MOULINEAUX. Of course. . . . Good-bye, mother-in-
law. (*He accompanies her outside the door.*)

SUZANNE. Good-bye, Madame.

MOULINEAUX. (*Still in hallway.*) Good heavens! (*He
drags* MADAME AIGREVILLE *back into the room.*) Your

husband is coming back! (SUZANNE *runs out the door at Left.*)

MME. AIGREVILLE. Who is it? What's wrong?

MOULINEAUX. An emergency! Go in there with Madame Aubin. I wouldn't think of having you see this patient. It's too gory! (*He pushes her into room at Left.*)

BASSINET. (*To* MOULINEAUX *who is following the women into the next room.*) Shall I come in there too?

MOULINEAUX. No! You stay to meet him. He will ask for Monsieur Blob—that's me—Monsieur Blob! Now get this straight! Tell him anything—tell him I'm busy—that I'm in conference. . . . that's it! I'm in conference with the queen of—with the queen of—the queen of Greenland. (*He disappears.*)

BASSINET. He's gone completely mad! And he thinks *I'm* sick! The doctor should see a doctor!

AUBIN. (*Bursting in.*) It's me again! Is Monsieur Blob here?

BASSINET. (*Who has had his back to* AUBIN.) He can't be seen now.

AUBIN. (*Recognizing* BASSINET.) Oh, the doctor!

BASSINET. Yes, the doctor! You know, then? Why did you ask for Monsieur Blob? Anyhow, he's not available at the moment.

AUBIN. I didn't expect to see you here. I was speaking to Monsieur Blob about you a while ago. Do you take care of him?

BASSINET. (*Not understanding.*) Yes—I take care of *him*—he takes care of *me*.

AUBIN. Is he very sick?

BASSINET. (*While speaking he unbuttons* AUBIN'S *vest as* AUBIN *rebuttons*.) You noticed it too? I think he has bugs in the brain.

AUBIN. What do you recommend for it?

BASSINET. Cold showers—that's the only thing. (*Unbuttons* AUBIN'S *vest again.*)

AUBIN. (*Slipping away and rebuttoning.*) Since I have you here, I'd like to talk to you about myself.

BASSINET. Fire away!

AUBIN. My blood doesn't circulate properly. I have frequent nosebleeds.

BASSINET. Very interesting. Is it painful?

AUBIN. I spoke to your butler about it and he told me some strange things.

BASSINET. You should try massages.

AUBIN. I tried that—it didn't help.

BASSINET. You didn't go about it right. You must choose a big, husky masseur—have him undress and stretch out on a table—then you massage him with all your strength for an hour. If your blood doesn't circulate after that, you need a transfusion.

AUBIN. I'll try it. I can see I've been going about it backwards. But back to the other matter. May I see Monsieur Blob?

BASSINET. (*With an air of mystery.*) Oh, no. . . . He's in conference—with the Queen of Greenland.

AUBIN. (*Amazed.*) The Queen—you say?

BASSINET. The Queen of Greenland.

AUBIN. Oh, la, la! He's top drawer, that dressmaker. No wonder his prices are so high. Queens, no less.

BASSINET. Perhaps you can come back another day.

AUBIN. Impossible. I want to tell him that I am bringing him a client, Madame Saint-Anigreuse—a friend of mine. It was her idea to go to my wife's dressmaker. I came here first because I didn't want to risk having her run into my wife. That's why I came to see if she has left.

BASSINET. (*Unbuttoning* AUBIN's *vest.*) Oh, was that your wife who was here a few moments ago?

AUBIN. Yes.

BASSINET. And you allow her to go out all alone?

AUBIN. Oh, no—I came here with her. But tell me—do you think he'll be long with the queen?

BASSINET. You know how queens are—real queens.

MME. AIGREVILLE. (*Shouting Offstage.*) Leave me alone— I'm leaving!

BASSINET. (*Aside.*) The mother-in-law! I'm getting out

of here! (*He slips out the rear door without* AUBIN *seeing him.*)

AUBIN. Tell me, Doctor. (*He turns.*) Where did he go?

(MADAME AIGREVILLE *enters.*)

MME. AIGREVILLE. I'm leaving, I said.

AUBIN. Your Highness!

MME. AIGREVILLE. WHAT DID YOU SAY?

AUBIN. Should I say—Your Majesty?

MME. AIGREVILLE. You find me majestic? (*Curtsies.*) To whom have I the honor of—?

AUBIN. Anatole Aubin.

MME. AIGREVILLE. Oh, the husband of Madame Aubin. I saw her a few moments ago—a charming woman. How is your dermatitis?

AUBIN. I beg your pardon?

MME. AIGREVILLE. I said—how is your dermatitis?

AUBIN. I don't have anything of that sort.

MME. AIGREVILLE. I'm sorry. Perhaps you'd rather not talk about it. Au revoir, Monsieur.

AUBIN. (*Bowing.*) Your Majesty!

(MADAME AIGREVILLE *exits as* MOULINEAUX *comes in followed by* SUZANNE, *whom he quickly pushes back through the door when he sees* AUBIN.)

MOULINEAUX. Back you go!

AUBIN. (*Turning.*) What did you say?

MOULINEAUX. I said, "Oh, you're back."

AUBIN. Tell me—has my wife left?

MOULINEAUX. A long time ago. She said that if you came back to tell you that she would be at the chiropodist.

AUBIN. That's perfect! I must tell you that a lady is coming to meet me here. I shouldn't like to have her encounter my wife.

MOULINEAUX. I see. A little intrigue, eh?

AUBIN. A very slight affair but just the same it would be best if my wife were left out of it.

MOULINEAUX. I understand. She might want to retaliate —is that it?

AUBIN. Impossible!

MOULINEAUX. (*Incredulous.*) Yes?

AUBIN. I have a delicate touch. All my life I've had affairs with married women. I could write a book on the subject.

MOULINEAUX. Yes?

AUBIN. Yes. I'm not like a lot of idiot husbands. Can you imagine, there was one husband who came with his wife to all our rendezvous? She told him she was going to see a fortune teller. (*He laughs.*) I was the fortune teller! I told her fortune while the husband waited outside. (*He is convulsed with laughter.*)

MOULINEAUX. (*Also laughing, slaps* AUBIN *on the shoulder.*) There aren't many husbands as stupid as that!

AUBIN. Besides, my wife wouldn't dare deceive me. She knows what I would do.

MOULINEAUX. What?

AUBIN. (*Going to him, points finger.*) BANG! BANG!

MOULINEAUX. That gives me the creeps.

AUBIN. But I didn't come to talk about that. You're going to be very happy when I tell you I'm bringing you a client.

MOULINEAUX. A client? For what?

AUBIN. For dresses, gowns, coats—anything you like.

MOULINEAUX. You think I have nothing else to do? What about my medicine? (*He realizes his blunder.*) The medicine that mad doctor gave me causes my eyes to blur. Sometimes I can't even see the needle.

AUBIN. I never heard of a businessman complaining about more business. Is it perhaps because you make gowns for crowned heads?

MOULINEAUX. What kind of gowns are those—for heads?

AUBIN. Well—you're either a dressmaker or you're not.

MOULINEAUX. If I wasn't, I'd be dead— (*Laughs.*) from starvation, you see.

(AUBIN *sits on sofa, laughing, as* MADAME HEBERT *comes in timidly.*)

MME. HEBERT. I thought you might not be so busy now and could talk to me about my jacket.

MOULINEAUX. Come in, my dear lady.

MME. HEBERT. I'm glad you're in a better mood. You see, the jacket is too large. No doubt you're the one who cut it. I wish you would re-cut it.

MOULINEAUX. Me?

MME. HEBERT. As soon as possible. I need it badly.

MOULINEAUX. I should cut it?

AUBIN. Why, yes—you're the dressmaker—you cut it.

MOULINEAUX. Of course, of course—I'm the dressmaker. . . . You want me to cut it. (*He grabs a big pair of shears and starts towards* MADAME HEBERT.) We'll just do that!

MME. HEBERT. (*Horrified.*) What are you going to do?

MOULINEAUX. You want me to cut it, don't you?

MME. HEBERT. Not now! I just want you to see what it needs and you can send for it tomorrow. (*Coyly.*) Only, I don't live where I used to—I live one floor higher. Goodbye, sir. (*She exits.*)

MOULINEAUX. Thanks for the information! (*He opens and closes the shears in a complete daze.*)

AUBIN. You get excited too easily. Do you know what someone recommended for you? Cold showers.

MOULINEAUX. Me? Who said that?

AUBIN. Doctor Moulineaux.

MOULINEAUX. (*Jerking his head, thinks for a moment he has lost his reason.*) MOULINEAUX!

AUBIN. Yes—the doctor I was talking to not ten minutes ago.

MOULINEAUX. You were talking to him? (*After a moment.*) Are you sick?

AUBIN. Why? Just because I saw the doctor? I met him quite by chance.

Moulineaux. This is getting too much for me. I'll have to think about it.

(Rosa *enters, a little dog in her hands*.)

Rosa. Oh—there you are!

Aubin. (*Going to her*.) Hello, my dear.

Moulineaux. (*Aside*.) Damn! And his wife is still here!

Aubin. Here is Madame Saint-Anigreuse whom I spoke to you about.

Moulineaux. Charmed! (*He puts his hand to his mouth in sign of surprised recognition*. Rosa *does the same*.)

Aubin. Here is a client worthy of you, Madame Saint-Anigreuse—the most aristocratic lady on the boulevards.

Rosa. (*To* Aubin.) My dear—Fifi is getting restless. I'm sure she needs to go out. Will you take her for a walk?

Aubin. Certainly not!

Rosa. What did you say?

Aubin. I said, "Certainly, my love." (*Reluctantly takes the dog and goes out with it*.)

Rosa. (*Opening her arms*.) Bubu!

Moulineaux. Rosa Pichinette! (*They embrace*.)

Rosa. Who would believe I'd ever see you again. It's been years.

Moulineaux. Yes—I was studying medicine.

Rosa. Did you ever get your degree?

Moulineaux. Of course—can't you tell? (*He struts around the room, hands behind back*.)

Rosa. But you became a dressmaker?

Moulineaux. (*After a thought*.) Huh? Oh, yes—to make my existence a little more colorful. The life of a doctor is drab, you know—routine sort of thing. But a dressmaker finds glamor and variety.

Rosa. Good old Bubu!

Moulineaux. Sh! Not so loud.

Rosa. Is there a sick person in the house?

MOULINEAUX. No—but there's no need of shouting "Bubu" like that. I'm not "Bubu" any longer.

ROSA. But I never knew you by any other name. What is your name now?

MOULINEAUX. Mou— I mean— BLOB!

ROSA. That's a silly name!

MOULINEAUX. I think so too. But it suits me.

ROSA. (*Strutting.*) Well—if you're not Bubu any longer, I'm not Rosa either. I'm Madame Saint-Anigreuse.

MOULINEAUX. Have you settled down?

ROSA. First I got married. To an imbecile.

MOULINEAUX. Naturally.

ROSA. Finally I deserted him—for a general.

MOULINEAUX. A general? That's a rare bird. Where did you find him?

ROSA. In a park—while my husband had gone to buy some cigarettes.

MOULINEAUX. Somebody else told me a story like that —only it was a cigar instead of cigarettes. (*A SOUND of things being broken in the next room.* MOULINEAUX *gets up and goes to the door.*) Oh, la, la!

ROSA. What was that noise? Have you an animal in there?

MOULINEAUX. Yes—an ostrich. I had it shipped here from Africa. I use the feathers, you see.

ROSA. (*Rising.*) Oh—let me see him.

MOULINEAUX. Oh, no—you can't. The stupid beast kicks everybody who comes near him. He's a vicious brute. But tell me, speaking of animals—I mean—your husband—you haven't ever seen him again?

ROSA. Never, thank heaven! I got away from him, thanks to his love of tobacco. Once I was free, I took the name of Madame Saint-Anigreuse and started a new life. (*New NOISES Offstage.*) Your ostrich is kicking up his heels again.

MOULINEAUX. Wait—I'm going to give him a piece of my mind.

Rosa. A lot of good that will do. You should pluck out all his feathers.

Suzanne. (*She bursts in, furious.*) HOW LONG ARE YOU GOING TO MAKE A FOOL OF ME? (*She stops abruptly, seeing* Rosa.) WELL! THIS IS TOO MUCH!

Rosa. Who is that woman?

Moulineaux. (*In a low voice.*) Nobody—she's the cashier. She has a bad nervous condition. Don't pay any attention to her. (*To* Suzanne.) Please calm down, Suzanne—no scandal.

Suzanne. (*Nervously.*) Why didn't you tell me you were with your mistress?

Rosa. Madame, what do you take me for? I'm a customer. I came here to be fitted for a dress.

Suzanne. You don't have to tell me stories like that. I know all about them.

Rosa. What?

Moulineaux. But I assure you—

Suzanne. You too? What kind of a moron do you think I am?

Rosa. If you're having an affair with your cashier you ought to spare your customers such scenes as this.

Suzanne. What cashier? What's she telling you?

Moulineaux. Nothing—it doesn't concern you.

Rosa. I am a lady, that is all. This man is my couturier.

Suzanne. Tell that to the woodpeckers.

Rosa. The proof is that I came here with my husband.

Suzanne. (*Affecting a laugh.*) Your husband! I'd like to see him!

Rosa. You shall see him—and shortly. He's walking my dog and should be back very soon.

Moulineaux. (*Crazed by the idea, grabs his brow.*) Oh, la, la, la, la, la!

Rosa. I hear him now. (*She goes towards the door and speaks to* Aubin *who enters with the dog.*) Tell this woman who I am. Tell her that you are my husband.

Aubin. I assure you— (*Recognizes* Suzanne.) My wife!

SUZANNE. (*Bolting.*) My husband!

MOULINEAUX. (*A long groan.*) Ohhh!

SUZANNE. I'll have my revenge! (*She exits in a whirl-wind.*)

AUBIN. Suzanne! Suzanne! (*To* ROSA.) Take this confounded dog! (*He tosses the dog to her.*)

ROSA. Anatole!

AUBIN. (*Pushing her away.*) Oh—go to the devil! (*He dashes out.*)

ROSA. (*The dog in her arms.*) How can he talk to me like that!!! OH, MY NERVES! I'M GOING TO FAINT! (*She falls limp into the arms of* MOULINEAUX *who takes the dog in one hand.*)

MOULINEAUX. Rosa—control yourself.

(YVONNE *enters.*)

YVONNE. Is Mother still here?

MOULINEAUX. (*Turning, finds himself face to face with* YVONNE.) Good God—my wife!

YVONNE. WHO IS THAT WOMAN? (*Starts to door.*) I NEVER WANT TO SEE YOU AGAIN AS LONG AS I LIVE! (*She rushes out.*)

MOULINEAUX. Yvonne—wait! I can explain everything.

YVONNE. (*Offstage.*) I don't want to hear it!

(BASSINET *enters.*)

MOULINEAUX. Will you take this woman and this damned dog! (*He pushes* ROSA *into* BASSINET'S *arms, hands him the dog and runs to the door.*) Yvonne! Yvonne! Wait for me! (*He rushes out.*)

BASSINET. (*Flustered at first, finally recognizes* ROSA.) I can't believe it. IT'S MY WIFE!!

(*He kisses her and* ROSA *opens her eyes for the first time since she fainted.*)

Rosa. My husband!

(She slaps him soundly on the cheek, grabs her dog and goes out in a spin as Bassinet *sinks on the sofa, totally confused and bewildered.)*

CURTAIN

END OF ACT TWO

ACT THREE

SCENE: *Same as Act One.*

AT RISE: *The Stage is empty. We hear a BELL ring, then there is a moment of silence, after which we hear* ETIENNE'S *voice Offstage.*

ETIENNE. That makes no difference, Monsieur.

MOULINEAUX. (*Coming out of door down Right, anxiously.*) Someone rang. Who is it? Etienne! Etienne!

ETIENNE. (*Appearing at rear.*) Monsieur?

MOULINEAUX. Who rang?

ETIENNE. (*Shrugging his shoulders.*) It was nothing.

MOULINEAUX. What do you mean—nothing?

ETIENNE. It was a sick man who came for an operation. He said: "Is the doctor in?" I said: "Yes." Then he told me he felt much better and he left.

MOULINEAUX. The idiot! Well, no matter! But in the future, when no one is there, please simply say, "It's no one, Monsieur."

ETIENNE. I thought that was useless.

MOULINEAUX. You can go now. (*He paces the floor, absorbed.*)

ETIENNE. (*After a pause.*) I can see that Monsieur is worried. I told you that your night at the Opera Ball was a bad thing. When inclined to do such things you must do them properly.

MOULINEAUX. What?

ETIENNE. Monsieur should have said to me: "Etienne, I am going to the ball." I would have slept in your bed.

MOULINEAUX. In my bed?

ETIENNE. Yes. I wouldn't have minded. I would have changed the sheets first. But it would have fooled your wife.

45

MOULINEAUX. Where is my wife? I wonder where she can be.

ETIENNE. That's what we were saying in the kitchen a while ago.

MOULINEAUX. In an hour it will be exactly twenty-four hours since she left.

ETIENNE. Oh, Monsieur, try to straighten things out, for my sake. I don't like to see people brooding. I'm very sensitive, Monsieur, and soon I'll be in the dumps myself.

(*A BELL rings.*)

MOULINEAUX. Someone rang!

ETIENNE. It's no one, Monsieur.

MOULINEAUX. What do you mean, It's no one"?

ETIENNE. No one can come in until I open the door. Right?

MOULINEAUX. All right, all right—go on.

ETIENNE. Thank you, Monsieur. (*He extends his hand, but seeing that* MOULINEAUX *does not respond, he shakes it in the air.*)

MOULINEAUX. And remember—outside of my wife, I'm at home to no one.

ETIENNE. No one?

MOULINEAUX. Not unless it's the Pope himself. No one!

(*He goes into his room,* ETIENNE *exits and comes back in with* AUBIN.)

ETIENNE. No, Monsieur, the doctor is not here.

AUBIN. But the porter downstairs said he was.

ETIENNE. The doctor told me two minutes ago that he isn't here. He should know better than the porter.

AUBIN. Yes? Well, tell him that Monsieur Aubin is here.

ETIENNE. He said no one unless it's the Pope. You're not the Pope.

AUBIN. No, but I must talk to him because of my wife.

ETIENNE. Well, he doesn't want to see anyone because of his.

AUBIN. Why is that?

ETIENNE. (*With importance.*) Things like that are the secrets of the master of the house. Their secrets concern only them—and their servants. And as for me, I am discretion itself. If you were to say to me: "Etienne, is it true that the household is upset, that the doctor didn't come home the other night, and that last night Madame didn't come home, and you're waiting for her?" I would say, "No, no, no—I don't know what you're talking about."

AUBIN. Oh, ho! You mean Madame Moulineaux didn't return to the marriage nest last night?

ETIENNE. How did you know?

AUBIN. You just told me.

ETIENNE. (*Indignant.*) Not me!

AUBIN. She didn't come home, eh? My wife either. I haven't seen her since yesterday's mix-up. It's unbelievable.

ETIENNE. (*Laughing stupidly.*) Your wife too? It must be contagious.

AUBIN. It won't go on forever. I know she'll come home. And besides, I had the idea of coming here. It's about this time she comes to see the doctor.

ETIENNE. But you know—the doctor is out to your wife as well as everyone else—at least until his wife comes back. (*BELL rings.*) Pardon me—someone at the door. (*He exits and then comes back in.*) Monsieur had better leave. Some ladies are here.

AUBIN. What ladies?

ETIENNE. Madame Moulineaux and her mother.

AUBIN. The doctor's wife? That's lucky! She came back.

(MADAME AIGREVILLE *enters with* YVONNE.)

MME. AIGREVILLE. MONSIEUR MOULINEAUX! (*To* ETIENNE.) Go tell him that Madame Aigreville is here.

AUBIN. Madame Aigreville? (*Bowing.*) Your Majesty!

ETIENNE. I'll tell him. He'll be very happy. (*He goes out door Right.*)

MME. AIGREVILLE. That would astonish me.

AUBIN. Your Majesty—Madame Aigreville. I don't understand. Then you are not—?

MME. AIGREVILLE. Not what?

AUBIN. The Queen of Greenland.

MME. AIGREVILLE. Me? You must also mistake the moon for green cheese, as they say.

AUBIN. Madame, I see that you are waiting for the doctor. Permit me to retire. (*Gestures to* YVONNE.) Madame! (*He goes out.*)

MME. AIGREVILLE. Queen of Greenland! His dermatitis must be making him have hallucinations. (*To* YVONNE.) Now remember—no weakness.

YVONNE. Don't worry, Mama.

MOULINEAUX. (*Entering.*) Yvonne! I've been on pins and needles. (*He starts towards her.*)

MME. AIGREVILLE. (*Blocking the passage.*) Back! NOT ANOTHER STEP!

MOULINEAUX. What do you mean?

MME. AIGREVILLE. Don't be led astray by our presence here.

MOULINEAUX. But—

MME. AIGREVILLE. You thought everything would arrange itself. Let me tell you, I know the duties that my role of mother imposes on me. I have brought back your wife.

MOULINEAUX. Thank you, mother-in-law—it was a good deed. (*He starts towards* YVONNE.)

MME. AIGREVILLE. (*Intercepting.*) Stop! It's not like you think. My daughter and I have discussed the matter at length, and this is what we have decided.

MOULINEAUX. Fine thing if your daughter listens to you!

MME. AIGREVILLE. You and your wife will no longer have anything in common.

MOULINEAUX. (*A bitter laugh.*) SEE! WHAT DID I TELL YOU!

MME. AIGREVILLE. At first I thought she should come to live with me. But upon reflection I decided that she should live under the same roof with you for appearance's sake.

MOULINEAUX. I'm glad of that.

MME. AIGREVILLE. And I shall live with her.

MOULINEAUX. What?

MME. AIGREVILLE. To be her consultant and her protector.

MOULINEAUX. That's going to be very cozy.

MME. AIGREVILLE. We shall live entirely apart from you. Men on that side— (*She points Right, then Left.*) women on that side.

MOULINEAUX. And this room will be for mixed types?

MME. AIGREVILLE. Only this room will be a common meeting place.

MOULINEAUX. Yes—we can hold our business conferences here.

MME. AIGREVILLE. In this manner I intend to regulate our life here and promote harmony in this household.

MOULINEAUX. (*Bitter laugh.*) My compliments! But let me tell you one thing. YOU ARE COMPLETELY MAD! In the first place, what am I guilty of? Tell me, Yvonne—what complaints do you have?

MME. AIGREVILLE. Don't answer him, Yvonne.

MOULINEAUX (*Furious.*) ARE YOU GOING TO LET HER SPEAK?

MME. AIGREVILLE. No scene, please.

YVONNE. You have the nerve to ask me what complaints I have?

MME. AIGREVILLE. A colossal nerve, I must say.

MOULINEAUX. I'M NOT TALKING TO YOU!

YVONNE. You speak more politely to my mother.

MOULINEAUX. Never mind that! WHAT COMPLAINTS?

YVONNE. I surprise you in a dressmaking shop with a woman slinking against your chest.

MOULINEAUX. She wasn't with me. Someone brought her there.

YVONNE. Is that why she was in your arms? Is that why you were hugging her?

MOULINEAUX. If you had looked carefully, you would have seen that I was NOT hugging her.

YVONNE. I tell you that you were hugging her and she was very pleased.

MOULINEAUX. Oh—she was pleased? That proves everything!

YVONNE. YOU CHASE AFTER DRESSMAKERS.

MME. AIGREVILLE. AND YOU INTRODUCE ME TO THEM AS IF THEY WERE YOUR PATIENTS.

MOULINEAUX. (*To* MME. AIGREVILLE.) The woman that you saw was Madame Aubin, wife of Monsieur Aubin —while the other one—

MME. AIGREVILLE. Was whose wife?

MOULINEAUX. Monsieur Aubin's.

MME. AIGREVILLE. Is Monsieur Aubin a bigamist?

MOULINEAUX. Yes—no—oh, you'll never understand. Why are you involving yourself in this? It doesn't concern you.

MME. AIGREVILLE. Doesn't concern me? Why, of all things!

MOULINEAUX. You're sticking your nose in my private life. I DIDN'T MARRY YOU! I owe explanations to no one but my wife.

MME. AIGREVILLE. Don't think for a moment that I would leave her alone in your clutches.

MOULINEAUX. In my clutches? (*He holds up his hands, monster fashion, and advances on his* MOTHER-IN-LAW, *backing her to the wall.*) AM I GOING TO SPEAK TO MY WIFE ALONE OR AM I NOT?

MME. AIGREVILLE. NO!

(MOULINEAUX *appears as if he is about to strangle her*

*but suppresses himself and stalks to the other side of
the scene.*)

YVONNE. Give in to him, Mama, so he'll have nothing
to reproach us for.

MME. AIGREVILLE. But I know you—you'll let him
wheedle you.

YVONNE. No I won't, Mama.

MME. AIGREVILLE. Very well. I'll leave. You can't say
I'm not reasonable. But you— (*She makes a face at him.*)
Uh! (*She goes out Up Left.*)

MOULINEAUX. (*Very calm, goes to* YVONNE.) Listen
Yvonne, forget for a moment that you have a mother and
believe me. Those two women are Monsieur Aubin's
secret, not mine. I don't even know them. I was called
there as a doctor. It's a very strange case—in pathological
medicine. I can't explain the details so you would understand. There's a lot of special study involved. But it's all
finished now, believe me. You surprised me in the middle
of an experiment. It didn't work, so I gave up the case .

YVONNE. All that's easy for you to say now.

MME. AIGREVILLE. (*Her head in the door.*) Are you
finished yet?

MOULINEAUX. NO! When we're finished we'll call you.

MME. AIGREVILLE. Don't believe a word he says, my
daughter. (*She disappears.*)

MOULINEAUX. She's a pest! (*Softly to* YVONNE.) Darling, everything I said was true.

YVONNE. If I could only believe you.

MOULINEAUX. But you must believe me.

YVONNE. It would be so nice to have confidence. But
you always lie to me.

MOULINEAUX. (*Aroused.*) Why do you say that?

YVONNE. Mama told me so!

MOULINEAUX. Your dear sweet mama told you.
THAT'S NO REASON!

YVONNE. Would you swear an oath?

MOULINEAUX. But—

YVONNE. To convince Mama. Swear that you are telling the truth.

MOULINEAUX. I swear to tell the truth, the whole truth and nothing but the truth, so help me Beelzebub!

YVONNE. Thanks. Then you really didn't know the woman I saw you with?

MOULINEAUX. If you ever see me with her again you can believe anything you like. Am I forgiven?

YVONNE. Not yet—later—when Mama leaves.

MOULINEAUX. Kiss me, at least.

YVONNE. That's another matter.

(*They kiss as* AUBIN *appears.*)

AUBIN. (*Aside.*) The dressmaker! With the doctor's wife! (*He remains at the door and listens.*)

MOULINEAUX. You're an angel!

YVONNE. Will you promise to slip into my room every night?

(AUBIN *is scandalized.*)

MOULINEAUX. I promise. (*Kisses her again.*)

YVONNE. And you won't stay away a whole night like you did?

MOULINEAUX. I promise. You'll have nothing to reproach me for.

YVONNE. But you've been a bad husband and you haven't loved your wife.

MOULINEAUX. It's you who don't love your husband.

AUBIN. (*Clearing his throat loudly.*) I was just coming in.

MOULINEAUX. Aubin—it's you. May I present Madame Moulineaux?

AUBIN. Yes, I know. I saw. (*He smiles.*) Lucky fellow!

MOULINEAUX. What?

AUBIN. Aside from that, how are things going? Have you started my wife's gown yet?

YVONNE. What gown?

MOULINEAUX. (*Very off-hand.*) Oh, nothing much—a gown I recommended for his wife—for her health.

YVONNE. Health?

MOULINEAUX. Yes, you know—a homeopathic gown—with electric wiring—very scientific.

YVONNE. That sounds fishy to me.

MOULINEAUX. Now don't start getting ideas in your head. You know that I love you more than anyone in the world.

(*He kisses her as* BASSINET *comes in.*)

AUBIN. The husband! (*He makes desperate signs to* MOULINEAUX, *who doesn't see him.*)

MOULINEAUX. I repeat. . . . I love you . . . I love you. . . . I love you.

BASSINET. A charming couple!

AUBIN. Monsieur Blob!

(*He is still waving frantically to* MOULINEAUX *who finally notices and waves back before kissing* YVONNE *again.*)

YVONNE. Not in front of all these people.

MOULINEAUX. I don't mind if you don't. (*He kisses her.*)

BASSINET. (*Taps* MOULINEAUX *on shoulder and speaks with comic gravity.*) I'm here, you know.

AUBIN. (*Front.*) This is going to be terrible!

MOULINEAUX. (*To* BASSINET.) What did you say?

BASSINET. I said you didn't even say hello to me.

MOULINEAUX. Oh! Hello!

AUBIN. And that's all? (*To* MOULINEAUX.) Monsieur Blob!

YVONNE. (*Low.*) Why does he call you Blob?

MOULINEAUX. Did he call me that? Some sort of a joke I suppose. He's very uneducated. Let's get out of here!

(*Aloud.*) I think I hear your mother calling you, dear. Let's go see what she wants. (*To the* OTHERS.) I'll be back before too long.

(*He goes out with* YVONNE. *There is a moment of silence then* BASSINET *points to the door where the couple went out and laughs lewdly.* AUBIN *joins in laughter.*)

AUBIN. You don't seem to care.

BASSINET. About what?

AUBIN. Oh, nothing.

BASSINET. (*Still laughing.*) I think we disturbed them.

AUBIN. Yes! (*A pause as he looks at* BASSINET.) What century are you living in?

BASSINET. They make a nice couple.

AUBIN. Nice couple! Monsieur, I'm no prude, but I don't understand why you don't pay more attention to your wife.

BASSINET. Give me time. I just found her yesterday.

AUBIN. You just found her?

BASSINET. Yes. She deserted me.

AUBIN. For the dressmaker?

BASSINET. No—for a soldier. I looked everywhere for her, but yesterday when I wasn't looking for her at all, I found her in the arms of—guess who?

AUBIN. Monsieur Blob.

BASSINET. Blob—that's right. How did you know?

AUBIN. It wasn't hard to guess.

BASSINET. When she saw me, she was so overcome that she slapped my face. I'm very happy about it.

AUBIN. Beaten and happy. That doesn't surprise me.

MOULINEAUX. (*Entering.*) It's all taken care of. I put some sense into my mother-in-law's head. (*To* BASSINET.) I beg your pardon, I was slightly occupied when you came in.

BASSINET. I understand—as long as you enjoyed yourself.

AUBIN. (*Taking* MOULINEAUX *by arm and going Left*

ACT III   A GOWN FOR HIS MISTRESS   55

with him.) I'd like to have a word with you. (BASSINET *follows in order to listen.*) I beg your pardon!

BASSINET. Don't mind me.

AUBIN. This is personal.

BASSINET. Oh! (*He goes to table, sits down and picks up a book.*)

AUBIN. (*Low.*) I wanted to tell you that I'm waiting for my wife. She usually consults you about this time and since I haven't seen her since yesterday—

MOULINEAUX. Damn!

AUBIN. I said "damn" too but it didn't help. I've got to make up some story about Rosa. You won't give me away, will you?

MOULINEAUX. Of course not. Husbands must stick together.

AUBIN. I will say that Rosa is your mistress.

MOULINEAUX. A good idea! No—good God! Wait! That won't work at all.

AUBIN. But she's the only one who would have to know. Please, Monsieur Blob, help me out.

MOULINEAUX. I couldn't do it. What if Madame Moulineaux found out? Ask someone else.

AUBIN. But who?

MOULINEAUX. I don't know. (*Notices* BASSINET *who is humming to himself.*) Try him.

AUBIN. Him? But what would Madame Moulineaux think if she found out?

MOULINEAUX. What difference would that make to him?

AUBIN. Oh, I see—no morals whatsoever! Well, I'll try it.

MOULINEAUX. (*To* BASSINET.) Monsieur Aubin has something to ask you. (*He walks away.*)

AUBIN. Yes—you can do me a great service.

BASSINET. Me?

AUBIN. Yes, I need a big favor.

BASSINET. Well, you see, it's so close to the end of the month. I'm a little short myself.

AUBIN. This won't cost you a cent.

BASSINET. In that case—fire away.

AUBIN. I'm in a tight spot with my wife at the moment. She caught me with my mistress.

BASSINET. (*Laughing naively.*) That was rather stupid of you, wasn't it?

AUBIN. (*Laughing in compliance.*) Stupid—yes! In a word, she's going to be here any minute. You know my wife. Well, I simply want you to tell her that Madame Saint-Anigreuse is YOUR mistress.

BASSINET. Well, now—that's an idea.

AUBIN. Yes!

BASSINET. But it's a bad one!

AUBIN. You're not going to refuse me, are you?

BASSINET. I certainly am.

MOULINEAUX. (*Coming over and whispering to* BASSINET.) Better accept. He's president of several companies and he can use a building or two.

BASSINET. (*Extending his hand to* AUBIN *quickly.*) On second thought, I accept. Tell me—is she pretty?

AUBIN. Who? Oh! Yes! Very pretty.

BASSINET. (*Laughing.*) And frisky?

AUBIN. Enough.

BASSINET. (*Laughing and punching* AUBIN.) A real chick, eh?

AUBIN. The best. Here's her photograph. (*He takes a photo from his wallet and hands it to* BASSINET.) You can show this to my wife to prove that you're telling the truth.

ETIENNE. (*Coming to door.*) Madame Aubin!

AUBIN. Quick—get that out of sight! (*He grabs the photo and shoves it into* BASSINET'S *coat pocket.*) Whew! That was just in time.

(ETIENNE *goes out.*)

MOULINEAUX. (*Crossing to* SUZANNE, *who has just entered.*) Bonjour, Madame.

AUBIN. (*Timidly.*) Bonjour, my dear Suzanne.

SUZANNE. Oh—you're here! In that case I'll leave immediately.

AUBIN. Listen to me, Suzanne! I swear that I'm innocent.

SUZANNE. You can tell that to the court when the time comes.

AUBIN. To the court? I won't hear of it. Now listen to me. It was all the result of a misunderstanding. You surprised me with a woman—yes. But I don't even know her. She belongs to this gentleman. (*To* BASSINET.) Isn't that so?

BASSINET. Oh, yes, yes, yes, yes.

AUBIN. You see?

SUZANNE. Tell that to someone else!

MOULINEAUX. Don't be too cruel, Madame. Someday *you* may want to be forgiven.

AUBIN. Please believe me, dear. I swear that you were mistaken. (*Low, gesturing to* BASSINET.) The photo—now!

BASSINET. Oh, yes.

(*He gropes in his pocket as* ETIENNE *enters with* ROSA.)

ETIENNE. Madame Bassinet is here.

BASSINET. (*Goes quickly to meet her.*) Good—she's arrived.

SUZANNE. Heavens! My husband's mistress!

BASSINET. (*Presenting* ROSA *to* AUBIN.) May I present—?

AUBIN. (*Who hadn't noticed* ROSA. *He lets out a groan.*) Oh—I just thought of something I must do. (*He rushes out Down Right.*)

BASSINET. What got into him? (*To* MOULINEAUX.) Moulineaux, I'd like to present—

MOULINEAUX. (*Raising his head.*) Oh—! (*He rushes out the Left door.*)

BASSINET. What's wrong with them all?

ROSA. I have no idea! But they're certainly not very polite.

BASSINET. Don't pay any attention. It's the surprise. (*Going to* SUZANNE.) Madame, may I present my—?

SUZANNE. No, you may not! (*Icily, she goes out Up Right.*)

ROSA. Another one! The nerve!

BASSINET. Perhaps she didn't understand me. (YVONNE *appears Up Left.*) Here's the lady of the house. Madame, allow me to present—

YVONNE. (*Stupefied, to* ROSA.) YOU HERE? (*To* BASSINET.) Well, Monsieur, I see you're still plying your trade. (*In a whirl, she goes out Up Left.*)

ROSA. (*Furious.*) This is beginning to be insulting!

BASSINET. (*Good fellow.*) Oh, no. It happens to me all the time.

ROSA. Well! Do something about it! Tell them who I am!

BASSINET. Wait—I'll tell them—all of them!

(*He goes to door where* YVONNE *exited and knocks. At this moment* MOULINEAUX *comes in door Down Left, and thinking* ROSA *is alone, runs to her.*)

MOULINEAUX. Why did you come here? Are you mad?

ROSA. Why? I'm with my husband.

MOULINEAUX. Your husband? Where?

ROSA. There—Bassinet. He found me yesterday.

MOULINEAUX. (*Pointing at* BASSINET. *Unbelieving.*) You mean—Bassinet?

BASSINET. (*Coming between them.*) What did you say?

MOULINEAUX. Nothing! (*He bursts into laughter.*)

AUBIN. (*Entering from Right and rushing to* ROSA.) Rosa—in the name of heaven—no scandal. Go away. My wife is here.

ROSA. You irritate me—all of you.

BASSINET. (*To* AUBIN.) Why do you have to whisper to her?

(YVONNE *and* MADAME AIGREVILLE *enter from Left,* SU-
ZANNE *from Right.*)

YVONNE. (*Arm in arm with* MAMA, *goes to* MOULI-
NEAUX.) Isn't this going a bit too far, Monsieur? Bringing
your dressmaker into your home.

MOULINEAUX. Huh? I wouldn't think of it. What dressmaker?

YVONNE. (*Pointing to* ROSA.) Her!

ROSA. Me?

MME. AIGREVILLE. (*Pointing to* SUZANNE.) NO!
HER!

SUZANNE. Me? (*She goes between* AUBIN *and* MOULI-
NEAUX.)

MOULINEAUX. You don't seem to agree on this.

AUBIN. (*Pointing to* SUZANNE.) But this lady is my
wife!

BASSINET. (*Showing* ROSA.) And this is my wife. And
I ask you to remember that when you talk about her.

ALL. His wife?

BASSINET. That is correct. My ever-loving wife.

AUBIN. His wife! Oh! (*Quickly to* BASSINET.) Give me
that photograph. I must have it.

BASSINET. Yes, yes—of course. (*He fumbles in his
pocket, draws out the photo and starts to look at it.*
AUBIN *tries to grab it.*)

AUBIN. Don't look at it! Give it to me!

BASSINET. (*Holding* AUBIN *away.*) Why shouldn't I
look at it? Don't be foolish!

AUBIN. (*Desperate.*) I insist!

BASSINET. (*Looking at photo.*) WELL!

AUBIN. (*Weakly.*) What?

BASSINET. It's funny, but this woman looks a little like
my wife. Don't you think so?

AUBIN. (*Very offhand.*) Oh, no—she's got too much—
uh—

BASSINET. (*To* MOULINEAUX.) Look at this. Don't you
think she resembles my wife?

MOULINEAUX. (*Pretending to study the photo.*) No—different eyes—and the cheek bones are too high.

BASSINET. (*To* ROSA.) What do you think? Does she look like you?

ROSA. Darling—how can you say that? I'm much prettier! (*She tears the picture into bits and hands it to her* HUSBAND.)

BASSINET. (*Stuffing the pieces in his pocket.*) You're right, my dear. It didn't look like you at all!

SUZANNE. (*To* AUBIN.) Then what you told me was true!

AUBIN. Yes! I've been trying to convince you for an hour.

SUZANNE. Oh, my dear Anatole, I'm sorry.

AUBIN. I forgive you.

YVONNE. (*To* MOULINEAUX.) And will you forgive me?

MOULINEAUX. No need to ask me that.

MME. AIGREVILLE. It's a good thing I'm here or it would all start again tomorrow.

YVONNE. My dear husband!

AUBIN. Her husband? But—I don't understand. . . . Then Doctor Moulineaux—?

MOULINEAUX. What about Doctor Moulineaux?

BASSINET. (*Pointing to* MOULINEAUX.) That's the doctor!

MOULINEAUX. (*Under his breath.*) Idiot!

AUBIN. And I thought you were a dressmaker.

MOULINEAUX. (*Quickly taking* BASSINET'S *arm and guiding him Downstage.*) Sh! I'll explain. My aunt was a dressmaker—the well-known Susie Blob. Surely you've heard of her.

AUBIN. Yes—perhaps I have.

MOULINEAUX. Well—when the poor dear thing died a few years ago, she willed her shop to me—but on condition that I run it.

AUBIN. Oh, I see. Why didn't you say so?

MOULINEAUX. I couldn't!

AUBIN. Why not?

MOULINEAUX. On account of my family. (*Very confidentially.*) You see—she was an illegitimate aunt.

(*In very friendly fashion, he escorts* AUBIN *back to the* OTHERS *and the CURTAIN comes down with the* THREE COUPLES *embracing while* MADAME AIGREVILLE *looks on, very pleased.*)

END OF THE PLAY

PROPERTY PLOT

Act One

Furniture appropriate to 1900 France:

1 sofa, left center
1 table, behind sofa
1 armchair, right of sofa
1 tabouret or hassock, front of sofa
1 flat-top desk, right
1 armchair, left of desk
1 straight chair, right of desk
1 cabinet with glass doors, right rear

DRESSING:

On desk are books and instruments a doctor might use. None
is specifically called for in the script
In cabinet are bottles of drugs and medical instruments
On wall, behind desk, diplomas in frames
In other parts of room, pictures, vases, bric-a-brac, ad lib

HAND PROPS:

Broom, duster, dust-pan (Etienne)
Real estate brochures and lease (Bassinet)
Calling card on tray (Etienne)
Suitcase and umbrella (Aigreville)
Woman's full-length glove (Yvonne)
White doctor's robe (Etienne)

Act Two

Furniture, typical of a dressmaker's salon:

1 sofa
1 armchair
2 straight chairs
1 long work table
1 clothes mannekin

DRESSING:

Shears, bolts of material, pin cushion and other dressmaker
equipment on table

HAND PROPS:
  Small poodle dog (Rosa)

Act Three

Same as Act One

HAND PROPS:
  Small photograph (Aubin)

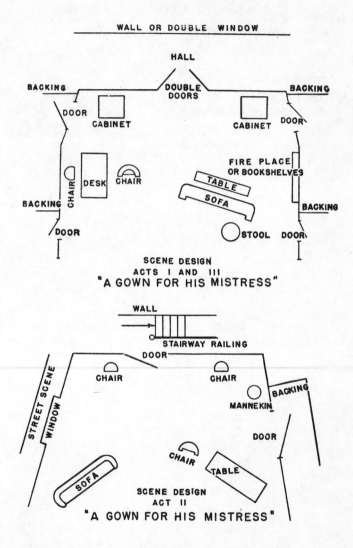

WALL OR DOUBLE WINDOW

HALL

BACKING   DOUBLE   BACKING
                           DOORS

DOOR
        CABINET   CABINET   DOOR

                                          FIRE PLACE
                                          OR BOOKSHELVES

        CHAIR   DESK   CHAIR   TABLE

BACKING   SOFA   BACKING

DOOR   STOOL   DOOR

SCENE DESIGN
ACTS I AND III
"A GOWN FOR HIS MISTRESS"

WALL

STAIRWAY RAILING

DOOR

        CHAIR   CHAIR
                                          BACKING
                              MANNEKIN

STREET SCENE
WINDOW   DOOR

                    CHAIR
        SOFA   TABLE

SCENE DESIGN
ACT II
"A GOWN FOR HIS MISTRESS"

64